The Island of
Free Ice Cream

BRAVE
BOOKS

N
W E
S

DOM-A-TRON

THE OLD ISLANDS

Burrycanter

Doomsdome

UTOPIA

Freedom Island

WIGGAMORE WOODS

SUMA SAVANNA

Rushington

Hive Haven

Toke-A-Toke   Furenzy Park

Wonder Well

Capitol

RAKA RAIN FOREST

Mushroom Village

Deserted Desert

Mt. Avalerie

SkyTree

Snapfast Meadow

CAR-A-LAGO COAST

Starlotte City

Gray Landing

Home of the Brave

Welcome to **Freedom Island**, Home of the Brave, where good battles evil and truth prevails. It's up to you to defend our great nation. Help the animals of Rushington save their city by completing The BRAVE Challenge at the end of this book.

Watch this video for an introduction to the story and BRAVE universe!

Saga One: The Origins
Book 3

The Island of Free Ice Cream

Saga One: The Origins—Book 3

The Island of Free Ice Cream

Book Illustrations © 2021 by Ali Elzeiny
Map Illustration © 2021 by Ali Elzeiny

Published by BRAVE BOOKS
www.BRAVEbooks.us

ISBN: 978-1-955550-02-4 (paperback)

First edition published in The USA in 2021 by BRAVE BOOKS.

Printed in Canada.

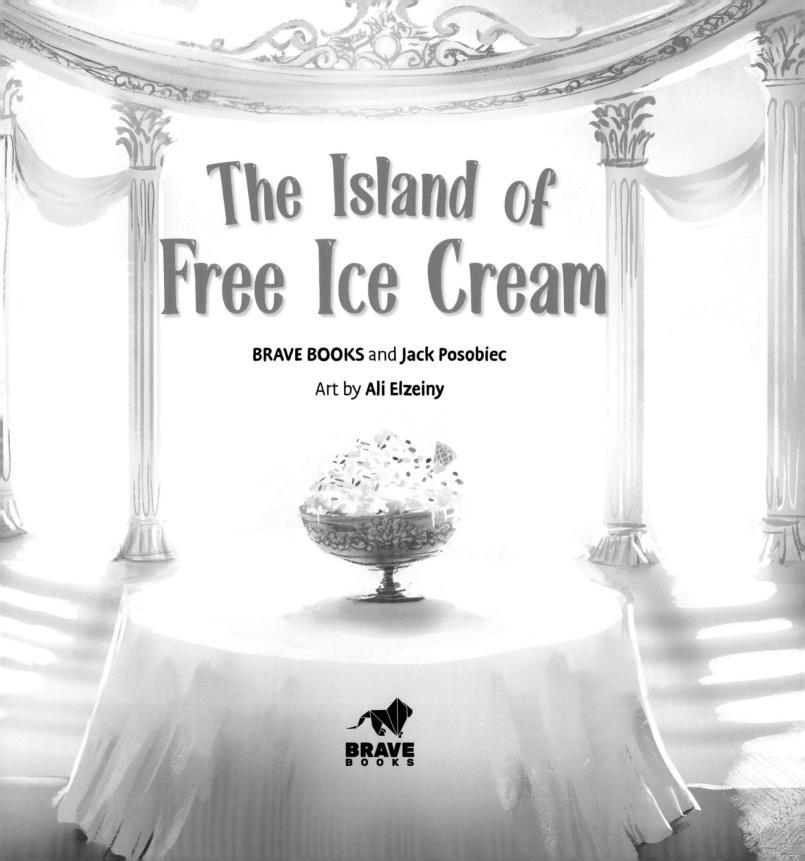

The Island of Free Ice Cream

BRAVE BOOKS and **Jack Posobiec**

Art by **Ali Elzeiny**

BRAVE
BOOKS

Rushington was the happiest city in all of Wiggamore
Woods. It hopped and popped, whizzed and whirled,
buzzing and bursting with all kinds of creatures.
The busiest spot of all was Rushington Market.

You could buy anything at the market: cookies, goodies, and gadgets galore. The animals of Rushington loved to buy and sell all sorts of things, but no one sold more than Asher the Fox.

Asher invented cranes for building,

tractors for plowing,

and special tape for fixing just about anything.

His finest invention was the freezer that let cows turn their milk into the most delicious ice cream you've ever tasted.

Because Asher's inventions made everyone's lives better, he had the biggest booth in the market. The animals of Rushington couldn't have been happier—until a pack of wolves came to town.

"You poor little animals," the wolves snarled. "Your market isn't fair! You all work so hard, but Asher has the biggest booth. We come from Utopia Island, which is so amazing that we don't even need a market—

FREE ICE CREAM FOR EVERYONE*

everybody gets the most delicious ice cream you've ever tasted FOR FREE. If you put us in charge, we'll make Rushington an even happier place to be."

Asher warned them that the wolves' promise sounded too good to be true, but the animals, drooling and dreaming of free ice cream, decided to vote. After Judge Cat-n-Paw counted the votes, Mayor Blendsynn declared that the wolves now controlled Rushington.

* Everyone who is a wolf

Then the wolves put Asher on a catapult and recited a chant:

"With a snap and a kick and a powerful swish,
You'll fly in the air and land with the fish."

And they launched Asher right out of Rushington.

Thankfully, Asher brought along his handy-dandy hang glider.

After gliding for two days and two nights, Asher landed on a strange and distant island. Animals hid in the alleyway shadows, and there wasn't a smile for miles.

Soon, Asher stumbled upon a long line of animals, where a dog named Pepper was very hungry.

"I'm so hungry, I could eat my pants," said Pepper.

Asher heard his stomach growl, too. "The wolves said that everyone in Utopia was full with free ice cream."

"Yes," agreed Pepper. "That's what the Council of Wolves promised, but they take all the ice cream for themselves. Now we can't buy or sell at the market, and all the wolves give us is this mushy, moldy macaroni."

Yuck!

Just then, a goat began to speak, "I can make food for the animals if you open the market and let me sell it! Hurry, before we all eat our pants!"

A wolf snarled, "A market won't make your tummies full. This goat must be punished for his lies."

The wolves recited their chant:

"With a snap and a kick and a powerful swish,
You'll fly in the air and land with the fish."

And they launched the goat out of Utopia.

One by one, the wolves slunk away from the crowd.
Curious, Asher and Pepper snuck in behind them.

"That went very well," sneered the top wolf. "Now, none of the animals will dare to speak up."

Another wolf chuckled. "When we've finished taking over Rushington and the rest of Freedom Island, everyone will be terrified of us and our catapults."

The Council shrieked and cheered, but Asher muttered, "Not if I can stop them." So he and Pepper set to work.

Asher built a secret submarine that he and Pepper used to escape Utopia and make their way to Toke-a-Toke.

There, a friendly singing elephant helped them carry a
cart of supplies to Rushington.

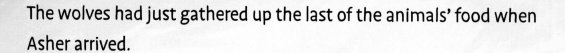

The wolves had just gathered up the last of the animals' food when Asher arrived.

"You took away the market that had everything we needed, and now we're starving!" said the animals. "When do we get ice cream?"

Asher leapt into action. "Animals of Rushington, the wolves are lying. They have stolen what you made, and they'll keep stealing everything you will make if you let them. I've been to Utopia, and guess what: there will be NO FREE ICE CREAM!"

"We don't want you to be in charge anymore," said the animals. "Let's vote!"

"Too late," growled the wolves.

"If you want your city back, you'll have to fight for it."

At last, Rushington was free. Judge Cat-n-Paw said the wolves were guilty of lying, and for their punishment, they were all loaded onto Asher's newest invention, a super-powered catapult.

The animals of Rushington recited a chant:

"With a snap and a kick and a powerful swish,
You'll fly in the air and land with the fish."

Rushington was safe at last. But when Asher received a mysterious letter, he knew this wasn't the end. Together, he and his friends set out to defend Freedom Island from lying wolves and other evil creatures.

Dear Asher,

What makes someone brave? Bravery is not ignoring danger or pretending it does not exist, but seeing it clearly and running to meet it.

Your passionate defense of Rushington City has come to our attention, and Son, you have our respect. Freedom Island needs defenders like you now more than ever. If you are willing to defend our dear island, answer the call. Journey to Wizards Way by the first day of fall.

Hurry. The world we love is under silent attack.

Anticipating your speedy arrival—
The Legends of Freedom Island

TO YOUR FAMILY

INTRODUCTION

BRAVE Books has created The BRAVE Challenge to drive home key lessons and values illustrated in the storybook. Each activity (a game and the accompanying discussion questions) takes between 10 and 20 minutes. Family-focused and collaborative, The BRAVE Challenge is a quick and fun option for family game night.

BRAVE CHALLENGE KEY

 Read aloud to the children

 One child modification

 For parents only

 Roll the die for the wolves

THE BRAVE CHALLENGE

 ## OBJECTIVE

Welcome to Team BRAVE! Your mission for this BRAVE Challenge is to defend Rushington from the wolves of Utopia by earning more BRAVE Bucks (BB) than the wolves. To get started, get a sheet of paper and a pencil, and draw a scoreboard labeled Team BRAVE vs. Team Wolves, like the one shown.

Team Wolves	Team BRAVE
|||	ⅢⅢ ||

While the children are creating the scoreboard be thinking about what they win if they defeat the wolves! Here are a few ideas:

- *Night out with parents*
- *Movie night*
- *Play the children's favorite game*
- *Ice cream*
- *Baking (and eating!) treats*
- *Bike ride*
- *Whatever gets your kiddos excited!*

 # WINNING

In this BRAVE Challenge, Team BRAVE will compete against Team Wolves to earn BRAVE Bucks (BB). At the end of all three activities, the team with the most BRAVE Bucks wins.

During each game, I (the parent) will roll a die for the wolves. The number rolled will represent the number of BB the wolves earned in that game. We will write this value on the wolves' half of the scoreboard.

As you follow the instructions, Team BRAVE will also earn BB. At the end of each game, we will write that value on the scoreboard under "Team BRAVE."

At the end, if Team BRAVE has earned more BB than the wolves, then you have successfully defended Rushington. The prize for winning will be _____. Let's begin!

INTRODUCING...
JACK POSOBIEC

Jack Posobiec is a popular influencer who has spent his career bringing awareness to issues close to his heart including the importance of family, faith, and the American way of life. He helped BRAVE Books write this story and The BRAVE Challenge and will be popping in to give you ideas on how you can explain these concepts to your child.

JACK SUGGESTS

"Hi, parents! I'm thrilled to be here with you during The BRAVE Challenge, and I hope you have as much fun playing the games as we did creating them."

GAME #1 - IN THE NAME OF FAIRNESS

LESSON Communism is not fair.

Communism: The government owns your things, only letting you use what they think you need.

MATERIALS NEEDED

Several sheets of paper, a hallway or long, open area, and a six-sided die.

Video Tutorial

OBJECTIVE

Welcome to Utopia Island! Team BRAVE, you have come to Utopia for The Greatest Paper Airplane Contest Of All Time. You will be battling against the Counsel of Wolves to see which team can make paper airplanes that go the farthest.

INSTRUCTIONS

1. Fold a paper airplane (one per team member).

2. Throw the airplanes down the hallway.

3. Count the number of steps from the starting line to the first team member's landed plane.

4. Repeat for all team members, adding the steps together.

5. **On the scoreboard, give Team BRAVE one BRAVE Buck (BB) for each step.**

 6. Roll the die (**Roll #1**) to determine the amount of BB the wolves earned in this game.

7. **Write this number on the wolves' half of the scoreboard.**

 Complete the above steps before continuing.

Before we move to discussion, we have a message from the Council of Wolves:

> "We the wolves hereby declare that it is not fair that Team BRAVE and Team Wolves earned a different number of BRAVE Bucks. So, instead of what you earned, each team will have exactly 10 BB."

Go to the scoreboard and scribble over the old scores. Give each team 10 BB.

But we're not done yet! Here's another message from the wolves.

> "Because we, the wolves, worked so hard to make both scores equal to ten, we think we should get a little extra reward. I'll take three points away from Team BRAVE and give three extra points to us."

Go to the scoreboard, and scratch out the numbers again. Give Team BRAVE 7 BB and Team Wolves 13 BB.

 BRAVE TIP

Gather all the paper airplanes and put them away before continuing so that they're not a distraction during the discussion.

TALK ABOUT IT

1. Just now, the wolves said they wanted to make everything fair, so they gave everyone the same number of BRAVE Bucks. How do you feel about that?

2. If you knew that you'd always earn the same number of points as the other team, would you ever try to do your best? Why?

3. When the wolves came to Rushington, they said that it wasn't fair that Asher had the biggest booth. Why do you think Asher had a big booth? (Hint: the text says why.) If Asher earned such a big booth, would the wolves be making the market better by taking the booth away from him?

4. In a communist country like Utopia, the people in charge say they make life fair by giving everybody the same reward, no matter what they earn. A person who works really hard would have the same house, car, and food as someone who doesn't work at all. Is this fair? What would it be like to live in a country like this?

 ### JACK SUGGESTS

The wolves in Utopia were supposed to take all the food and give everyone their fair share of ice cream—instead they took the good food for themselves and gave everyone else moldy, mushy macaroni. Talk to your children about the nature of man and how we all need limitations on power.

5. Now, in the game we just played, the wolves said they were going to make the points more fair, but then what did they do? How did you feel about that?

> "Let each of you look not only to his own interests,
> but also to the interests of others."
>
> **Philippians 2:4** (ESV)

6. If the wolves change the points like this in all the games we play today, who's going to win?

GAME #2 - WOLF TANK

LESSON Competition within a capitalist society leads to better products and services.

Capitalism: You own your own things, and you have the right to buy or sell what you want.

MATERIALS NEEDED

A timer and a six-sided die.

Video Tutorial

OBJECTIVE

We're back in Rushington, and guess what: you have a booth in Rushington Market! In this game, six animals will come to the market and explain their problems. You as Team BRAVE will compete against another seller to invent solutions to the animals' problems.

INSTRUCTIONS

1. Roll the die (**Roll #2**) and see how many bucks the wolves earned at the market.
2. **Record this number on the wolves' half of the scoreboard.**
3. I'll read a situation and explain what the other seller is offering.
4. You work as a team for sixty seconds to come up with a better solution.
5. Choose one person from your team to present your solution to me.
6. I'll tell you what the animals think.
   - If the animals like your solutions better than the other sellers', they'll pay you 2–3 BRAVE Bucks (BB).
   - If your answers are about the same as the other sellers', then you get 1–2 BB.
   - If they like the other sellers' answers better, then you get 0 BB.

7. When you earn BB, we'll record it on the scoreboard.

8. Repeat for the next situation with a different team member coming forward to present the solution and earn points.

Ready to beat the wolves? Here are the animals and their problems ...

Start the timer after reading each situation and let the kids discuss. When the timer goes off, have them choose one person to present their findings to you. Parents award 0–3 BRAVE Bucks as they see fit. **Record any BB they earn on the scoreboard.**

JACK SUGGESTS

Encourage your kids to be creative! Rather than awarding BB to the most practical answer, try to reward your kids for outside-the-box solutions. That's what makes a good entrepreneur.

1. A pizza delivery panda is trying to carry a pizza from Rushington to Toke-A-Toke, but he doesn't want to carry it in his hands the whole time. A kangaroo wants to sell the panda a fanny pack to stuff the pizza in. What will you sell him?

— **BRAVE TIP** —

Be generous with points to help team brave recover a slight lead after the last game. However, don't give your kids such a big lead that they lose interest.

---

2. Asher wants to hang glide over Mt. Avalerif, but he's afraid it will be too hot. A polar bear wants to sell Asher an ice cube to hold as he flies. What will you sell him?

3. Pepper wants to reach the very top of Sky Tree, but she thinks it will take too long to climb up the trunk like everyone else. A bunny wants to sell her a pogo stick. What will you sell her?

4. Farmer Goat is trying to get rid of the huge mountain of moldy, mushy macaroni left in Utopia. A hen wants to sell him a little broom and dustpan. What will you sell him?

TALK ABOUT IT

1. What did you get from helping these animals? What did they get from you?

JACK SUGGESTS

In a fair country, we earn money when we make or do things that help other people. It's a system that benefits everyone.

2. Can you think of any problems that you have in your life and the things your family buys to help you fix them? For example, how do you talk to your grandparents when they're not at your house? (*Phone*)

3. People who come up with and sell new ideas to help others are called *entrepreneurs*. If you were an entrepreneur, what problem would you solve, and what new idea would you come up with?

4. In Rushington, a fish opens a candy store that only sells candy made from icky-sticky seaweed. A bee opens a candy store that sells honey-flavored candy. Where would you rather shop? Why are options good?

JACK SUGGESTS

When people have the power to choose between many options, they force companies to compete to produce the best product at the lowest cost.

GAME #3 - SENSATIONAL SERVICE

LESSON   Capitalism incentivizes people to create value for others.

MATERIALS NEEDED

A couch or recliner and a six-sided die.

Video Tutorial

OBJECTIVE

I am a grumpy wolf who has come to Rushington for a spa day. You are workers at the spa I'm visiting, and your goal is to make me happy so that you can earn a good tip.

BRAVE TIP

Don't think that this game is just for moms! Dads can give their kids the chance to giggle by accepting this spa treatment too!

INSTRUCTIONS

All the team members will work together to accomplish the tasks on the list below. I'm going to be grumpy the whole time. You'll have to work very hard to make me happy by doing exactly what I ask. For each task, I'll give you either 0, 1, or 2 BRAVE Bucks (BB), depending on how well you serve me. Learn from the mistakes of other team members to earn more BB.

*Before starting, roll the die (**Roll #3**) to see how many BB Team Wolves earned for their tips.* **Record this number on the scoreboard.**

Choose one task below for the first BRAVE team member and start testing their customer service.

- Back massage
- Brush my hair
- Rub my feet
- Head massage

- Fan me to keep me cool
- Braid or tie up my hair
- Get me a robe
- Walk on my back

JACK SUGGESTS

Be assertive! Don't be afraid to push your kids' patience and even take back part of their BRAVE Bucks if the service is poor. This game should teach them how much customer satisfaction affects the success of a business in a free market country. Make sure to keep it competitive between Team BRAVE and Team Wolves so they don't get discouraged.

*After each child has tried, add their scores together. **Write that number on the scoreboard for Team BRAVE.***

TALK ABOUT IT

1. When you go to a spa, restaurant, or movie, how do you want the workers to treat you?

2. Was it easy to please me, the nasty wolf in the spa? Why did you try anyways?

3. Imagine the government said every worker at the spa will get two BB no matter how they treat customers. If you were working for grumpy customers when this happened, would you work hard to make them happy?

"Whoever is slack in his work is a brother to him who destroys."

Proverbs 18:9 (ESV)

4. How did the wolves treat the animals in Utopia? How did the animals treat each other in Rushington? Would you like to live in Rushington or Utopia?

TALLY ALL THE POINTS TO SEE WHO WON!

 # IN CLOSING

Today, we discussed how Asher had to deal with the Wolves from Utopia and save Rushington. What Asher was really dealing with was communism in Utopia versus capitalism in Rushington.

Communism: The government owns your things, only letting you use what they think you need.

Capitalism: You own your own things, and you have the right to buy or sell what you want.

In our games we discussed how communism isn't fair, how competition leads to better products and services, and how capitalism makes people want to create value for others.

Make sure to check out the previous books in this saga!

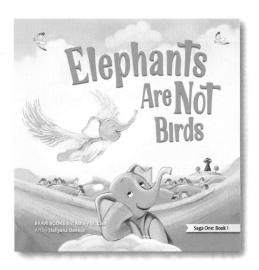 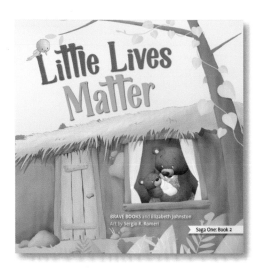

Elephants Are Not Birds: Kevin the Elephant has always loved to sing. When a vulture named Culture suggests that Kevin is actually a bird, he embarks on an adventure exploring reality, identity, and truth.

Little Lives Matter: Life is hard for Mobi and his mother, but love carries them through—until a vulture named Culture seeds a new idea: "Why don't you just live for yourself?" Follow Mobi as he learns the value of life at all stages.

Upcoming topics in this saga include: cancel culture, Critical Race Theory, the right to bear arms, truth, family, and more!

Visit www.BRAVEbooks.us to learn more today!